NiGHtBEAR

To Anna, Doffy and Blindeyes

Some other books by Rebecca Patterson:

My Big Shouting Day

My Busy Being Bella Day

NIGHTBEAR
A JONATHAN CAPE BOOK 978 1 780 08008 6

Published in Great Britain by Jonathan Cape, an imprint of Random House Children's Publishers UK
A Random House Group Company

This edition published 2014

1 3 5 7 9 10 8 6 4 2

Copyright © Rebecca Patterson, 2014

The right of Rebecca Patterson to be identified as the author of this work has been
asserted in accordance with the Copyright, Designs and Patents Act 1988.

RANDOM HOUSE CHILDREN'S PUBLISHERS UK,
61–63 Uxbridge Road, London W5 5SA

www.**randomhousechildrens**.co.uk
www.**randomhouse**.co.uk

Addresses for companies within The Random House Group Limited can be found at:
www.randomhouse.co.uk/offices.htm

THE RANDOM HOUSE GROUP Limited Reg. No. 954009

A CIP catalogue record for this book is available from the British Library.

Printed in China

The Random House Group Limited supports the Forest Stewardship Council®(FSC®),
the leading international forest-certification organization. Our books carrying the FSC label
are printed on FSC®-certified paper. FSC is the only forest-certification scheme supported
by the leading environmental organizations, including Greenpeace.
Our paper procurement policy can be found at www.randomhouse.co.uk/environment.

NIGHTBEAR

Rebecca Patterson

Jonathan Cape • London

I am not a new bear.
I am probably older than you!

And I have been around
a very long time.

I was born in a factory
somewhere up North.

Then I was a
birthday present . . .

for people who
never loved me.

And they put me in a bag with some old shoes
and **GAVE ME AWAY** to the charity shop!

I have been stuck here for years. Doing nothing. Feeling lonely and waiting for someone to buy me.

But the people who come into this shop **NEVER** want a bear.

I wait and wait. Someone must need a cute bear like me!

And if I sit on this shelf any longer my fur will get all flattened on my bottom.

But who's **THIS?**

She looks friendly.
I will do my **BEST** smile!

It worked!
She's patting me!

And
she's asking
her mum.
Oh please,
say yes!

Yes!
I **AM** in very good
condition for 50p.

SHE'S
BUYING
ME!

And now, I think, we're

GOING
HOME!

She says my name is Buttercup.
I hope that's a proper boy's name.

She has
SIX OTHER BEARS!

So I won't be lonely!

All the bears in this house have really important jobs.

They are busy working
ALL DAY!

EVERY DAY!

Tufts works the lift.
He pulls it up!
All by himself!

Mr Brownbear
has to dress up
like a **BABY!**
And go out in the
little buggy almost
every afternoon!

And Betty and Doffy
say they have a very
HARD job. They have
to put on big earrings
and dance!

But Frank says his job
is **MUCH** harder.

He has to do stunts!

She **THROWS** him up . . .

and **TWIZZLES** him about . . .

and makes him do

BIG FLIPS!

Babyblue says the
WORST JOB EVER
is helping her ride her bike!

And all of them have to do these beauty shows.

EVERY DAY!

Sometimes I wonder if **I** could get a job here. But Betty and Mr Brownbear say there are no jobs left.

I'm not highly skilled.

I wish I was.

Sometimes I feel a bit left out.

Well, these bears are **EXHAUSTED**
working all day for her!

As soon as they get back to bed, they

SLEEP AND SLEEP AND SLEEP!

I don't sleep! I'm not tired.

I stay **WIDE AWAKE**
and listen to all her stories.

And I am always awake
EVERY NIGHT,
ready to hug her if she has a

HORRIBLE DREAM!

Once she was sick at night.
And I was there to help.

I got some sick
on my head!

BUT I DIDN'T MIND!

So when these bears wake up, I tell them about the jobs **I** do in the night.

Now they know I am a **SPECIAL** bear . . .

I am . . .
NIGHTBEAR!